Squirrel Joins the Game

by Jay Dale

illustrated by Tamara Joubert

Today was a big day.
Luca's football team, the Gold Lions,
were playing the Grey Sharks.

The teams were about to play.
But a little grey squirrel
ran across the pitch.
It jumped over the ball
and then ran off the pitch.

2

Everyone laughed.

Luca turned to his friend, Ky.
"Maybe the squirrel wants to be
on our team," he smiled.

The referee blew her whistle
and the game began.

But just as Luca was about to kick
the ball, the squirrel came back.
This time it ran up the goal post
and stayed at the top.

"Stop play!" shouted the referee.

"Looks like the squirrel wants
to join the game," laughed Jilly.
Jilly played for the Grey Sharks.
She was their best player.

"Looks like it!" smiled Luca.

Just then, the referee came over.
"We can't play while a squirrel
is on the goal," she said.
"Someone has to move it."

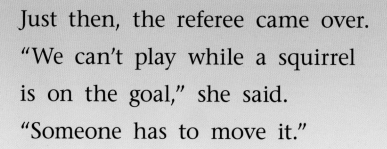

The mums and dads
walked onto the pitch.
Everyone looked at the squirrel.
It rubbed its little paws
as it stood on top.

"We have to catch it," said Luca.

"But how?" asked Jilly.

Luca's dad got his phone out.
"It says here that squirrels
love peanut butter.
We should put some in a cage to catch it."

"I have a peanut butter sandwich,"
said Ky.
"We could try to catch it
with my sandwich."

"But we don't have a cage,"
said Luca.

"Oh, yes we do!" smiled Jilly.
"My mum is a vet,
and she has a cage in her van."

9

Jilly ran over to the van
and got the cage.
And Ky got his sandwich.

Luca looked at the little grey squirrel.
It stayed very still –
as if it was waiting
for the game to begin.

Jilly put the cage down.
And Ky put his sandwich inside.

The squirrel sniffed.
Then, all of a sudden,
it ran down the post
and into the cage.

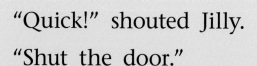

"Quick!" shouted Jilly.
"Shut the door."

"Got you!" said Luca.
But the squirrel didn't look up.
It was too busy eating Ky's sandwich!

After the game, Luca, Ky and Jilly
carried the squirrel to the park.
They opened the cage door,
and it ran towards a tree.

Then it stopped and looked back
at the children.

Luca laughed.

"I think our little friend is saying 'thank you' for the game.

And for the peanut butter sandwich!"